SHARK DOG

SCHOOL TRIP

and the School Trip Rescue!

Ged Adamson

HARPER

An Imprint of HarperCollinsPublishers

ISBN 978-0-06-245718-9

The artist used pencil and watercolor paints to create the illustrations for this book.
Typography by Jeanne Hogle
18 19 20 21 22   SCP   10 9 8 7 6 5 4 3 2 1
❖
First Edition

For Jay, Zsuzsanna, Vincent, and Sasha

You won't meet many pets like Shark Dog.
He's sort of a dog, but he's also kind of a shark.
Life with him is a great big adventure.

My dad is a famous explorer, so Ms. Ablett invited him along on our class trip.

We would be exploring the great outdoors! Of course, it made sense for Shark Dog to join the fun.

Things got off
to a perfect start.

CLICK!

CLICK

CLICK

"Say cheese, Shark Dog!"

We followed a trail to a beautiful pond.
"Just look at all those frogs and toads,"
said Ms. Ablett.

"They're enjoying the sunshine," said my dad.

But not for long.

"Shark Dog! No!"

Everyone agreed that this wasn't going to be an ordinary school trip.

There was so much to
see on the nature trail.

After hours of exploration, it was finally time to stop for lunch.

Suddenly, it began to rain.

And with rain comes mud.

Shark Dog loves mud!

What a mess!

Once the rain had stopped, the sun was shining again.
My dad told everyone to find a partner and explore together.

"Be on the lookout for something interesting, and
we'll meet back here in thirty minutes," said Dad.

We all shared our discoveries.

skunk

owl

But there was one discovery that got everyone's attention.

Footprints.

BIG footprints!

Shark Dog's nose began to twitch.
"What is it, boy?" asked Dad.

"Everybody follow Shark Dog!"

"Are you sure this is a good idea?" I asked.

Shark Dog came to a sudden stop.
Somebody was in trouble.

"We need to help him!" I yelled.

But Shark Dog was already one step ahead.
He grabbed the tree trunk. We all joined in.

"1,
2,
3,
LIFT!!!"

The bear cub was okay, thanks to Shark Dog!

After a slobbery thank-you,
he bounded back into the woods.

"Oh no. With all this excitement, we've gone way off the path," said Ms. Ablett.

Our teacher was right.
But in an instant, Shark Dog was off again!

FOLLOW THAT SHARK DOG!!

Shark Dog's nose
led us back to the bus.

We all agreed this was no ordinary school trip.
Because of Shark Dog, it was even better!